holiday

a minedition book
published by Penguin Young Readers Group

Thank you Léonie for the beginning of the story. G.E.

Text copyright © 2006 by Géraldine Elschner
Illustrations copyright © 2006 by Angela Kehlenbeck
Original title: PASHMINA, das Weihnachtszicklein
Coproduction with Michael Neugebauer Publishing Ltd., Hong Kong.
Rights arranged with "minedition" Rights and Licensing AG, Zurich, Switzerland.
All rights reserved. This book, or parts thereof, may not be reproduced in any form
without permission in writing from the publisher,
Penguin Young Readers Group, 345 Hudson Street, New York, NY 10014.
The scanning, uploading and distribution of this book via the Internet or via any
other means without the permission of the publisher is illegal and punishable by
law. Please purchase only authorized electronic editions, and do not participate in
or encourage electronic piracy of copyrighted materials. Your support of the author's
rights is appreciated.
Published simultaneously in Canada.
Manufactured in Hong Kong by Wide World Ltd.
Typesetting in Veljovic book by Jovica Veljovic.
Color separation by Fotoreproduzioni Grafiche, Verona, Italy.

Library of Congress Cataloging-in-Publication Data available upon request.

ISBN 0-698-40046-1
10 9 8 7 6 5 4 3 2 1
First Impression

For more information please visit our website: www.minedition.com

Géraldine Elschner

PASHMINA

THE LITTLE CHRISTMAS GOAT

with pictures by Angela Kehlenbeck

minedition

It was winter. Snow blanketed the land, and in Simon's little house up on the mountain, a fire was burning continually in the stove.

The big celebration was getting closer. Tomorrow was Christmas and the children were excited, but Manja, their mother, was worried.

What would they eat on this special day? There were still potatoes from the garden and there were beans that Manja had dried, but that was all. She had so wanted to cook something special. A roast would have been nice or a lovely fish, which was the custom in so many homes.

She asked her husband to go and find something special, catch something, hunt something, fish something, anything. There just wasn't enough money to buy anything.

"Something special? You're a fine one!" he laughed.
But he buttoned his old jacket and disappeared into
the snow. Simon trudged his way through the fields,
through the woods, and up through the mountains.
But there was nothing. The lake was frozen over and
it was as if the earth had swallowed up all the animals.

"I can't come home empty-handed!" he brooded.
Suddenly he stopped where he was.
Was that a noise?
Had he just heard a soft whimpering?
There, under a thorn-bush...

Carefully, he freed the little goat from the thorny branches.

Then he put it inside his jacket and started on his journey back home.

"Where did you get that?" asked his neighbor, Old Martin, when he saw the little head peeking out of Simon's jacket.

"It was lying in the snow," explained Simon.

"What? Such a yummy roast on the side of the road?" said Martin. "What luck! Well, have a nice Christmas and enjoy your dinner!"

As soon as Simon pushed the door open,
Manja rushed toward him.
"And? Did you find something?"
she asked nervously.
"No," he said. "I mean yes, but…"
He took the little goat from his jacket and
laid it in front of the stove.

Just as he did, the children came storming in.

"Oh!" said Paul.

"What funny little ears!" added Leonie.

"Martin thought it would make a great Christmas dinner,"
said Simon taking a chance.

"WHAT?" cried the children.

Their parents just looked at them. Then they looked at the
goat. What should they do? Instead of a wonderful Christmas
dinner they would just have another hungry mouth to feed.

"Please, oh please, no," begged the children.

"Well, alright," said Simon and got a little box and filled it
with straw.

On Christmas Eve, they all enjoyed their beans
and potatoes.
"Delicious!" laughed Paul.
"Maaaa," agreed the little goat from under the
Christmas tree.

Simon laughed, and the whole family joined in.
They named the little goat Pashmina.

Soon Pashmina was jumping and climbing like all little goats, and was into everything you could imagine. She was frisky and funny and followed the children everywhere. However, one thing about the goat was very unusual.

Pashmina's soft, fluffy hair grew very quickly. And the hair was also curly and shiny and as white as the snow that covered the ground on that day before Christmas when Simon found her.

The children could pet her for hours and Pashmina would close her beautiful almond-shaped eyes and lay her head in their laps.

One spring morning, while petting Pashmina, Leonie suddenly jumped up and ran to her mother.

"Look!" she cried. In her hand she held what looked like a little white cloud.

"Oh, Pashmina is losing her winter coat," explained her mother.

But Pashmina was losing so much that Manja
was able to spin the hair into a wonderful
yarn. She knit warm socks for Simon and the
children. The rest she sold at the market in
the city.

With the money they earned, they bought a
young billy-goat. And five months later, Pashmina's
first little baby was born.

Now there was a little snow-white goat family living in the old shed.
Three became four, then five, six and seven. Soon there were many goats and Manja's mohair items became so well known throughout the area that Martin's daughter and other women from the village were helping her spin yarn and make clothing. The village now had its own little workshop.

Old Martin, who had become the goatherd,
told everyone who came into the little shop the
unbelievable story of how a little angora goat escaped
the cooking-pot "by just a hair."

Of all the goats in the herd, Pashmina's wool was the
most beautiful and plentiful. Could this be her way of
saying thank you for that very special Christmas Eve?